An Intelligent Life
by Robert Jameson

**Warning/Disclaimer**

Please take careful note that the fictional narrator in this book is a man of strong views, strong language and strong actions. If you do not wish to take the risk of being offended, now is the time to stop reading this and go and get on with some mindless texting or inane twittering - or whatever it is you do!

Please also be aware that this is a work of fiction. Nothing in this book should be interpreted as a reliable fact about the real world. Furthermore, neither the opinions expressed nor the experiences described by the narrator should be confused with the opinions or experiences of the author.

# Preface

The narrator and central character in this book has no name, but, for the sake of convenience, let's call him Jack.

For much of this book, Jack rants and launches into one diatribe after another about the state of the world and the shitty people he meets in it. If this isn't the sort of thing you want to read, that's fine, but please don't be so fucking thick that you read this book and then complain that it's full of rants and diatribes. Yes, it is! That's the idea! This book is for people who enjoy that sort of thing.

I enjoy Jack's diatribes because, sometimes, I feel like he does. When God saw fit to make me, however, he made me remarkably sanguine. I take the same shit Jack takes, yet remain calm. Somehow it barely bothers me at all. Actually that's not quite right - it does bother me; it bothers me a great deal how shitty people are to each other and how obstinately stupid they choose to remain - I just don't take it personally.

I look around and I see a world plagued by selfish stupidity. I see it as a serious problem that needs to be dealt with, but I don't see it as a personal punishment or as a judgement on my past lives. I manage to remain largely above the worst of all the hate and anger - but I think there's a Jack inside and I wonder what it is that contains him so well.... and whether that containment is foolproof.

The central character in this book has, as you will discover, a tendency towards violence. I am drawn to Jack. I like him. I'm interested by his ideas and by the frustrations and anger that he feels. I even share his sense of satisfaction when something nasty happens to someone who has been asking for it. I don't, however, advocate any such hatred or violence. I advocate kindness in all things. I wonder, nevertheless, how long it will be before Jack's methods and solutions are the only ones we have left.

# Contents

# Intelligence

It is so abhorrent to some people that anyone should be deemed to be more intelligent than anyone else, that they seek to distort the entire concept of intelligence and render it utterly meaningless. One way in which they do this is by describing all sorts of dubious 'qualities' as 'forms of intelligence.'

It's offensive, apparently, to suggest that any particular person might be less intelligent than anyone else. So, when someone is clearly not intelligent in any sort of traditional way, they are described as being 'intelligent' in some other way. They are assigned a made-up form of intelligence so that they don't feel left out.

A person with musical talents might be described as having 'musical intelligence.' It's a marvellous sort of talent to have, but why can't we just call them 'musical'? Why do they have to have 'musical intelligence'?

And does it mean anything to say that someone has 'artistic intelligence'? They might be able to conjure up a remarkable likeness of my Aunt Harriet, using nothing but a blunt piece of charcoal and a scrap of paper, but does that really make them intelligent? What's wrong with just being a 'talented artist'?

Even when a person has no discernible talents, qualities or usefulness whatsoever, they can still be intelligent, apparently! They might, for example, be - and this is the most damning of all forms of intelligence - 'emotionally intelligent.'

Admittedly, it can be difficult to define what exactly intelligence is. It might be variously described as an ability to think rationally, to make logical deductions, to make rational decisions based on a coherent set of values and principles or as an ability to conceptualise and solve problems - but what it fucking-well isn't is a tendency to obsess about your own or other people's feelings, pander to other people's sensitivities and fret about fitting in! Neither is it about being skilled in toadying up to people or having a desperate need to manipulate people into liking you. There is no such fucking thing as 'emotional intelligence'!

People can have other qualities - very important, admirable qualities - that are not dependent on them being intelligent. They can be reliable, patient or generous - but these aren't forms of intelligence.

As for being emotionally intelligent: Do me a fucking favour! It's little more than a term to describe witless, oversensitive, conformist pricks, too afraid of upsetting their own or other people's feelings to have anything interesting to say for themselves. Emotional intelligence? Fuck right off!

The reality is that intelligence is not a quality that is equally distributed - not even in different forms. Most people are not intelligent - their lives are not coordinated through rational thought.

Intelligent people are few and far between and the explanation for how they became so much more intelligent than the rest of the population is an interesting one. It is simply that they were the only ones who could actually be bothered to work at it. It turns out that thinking is something you have to practise if you want to be good at it. Who would have guessed?

Real intelligence is born of dedication to the art of thinking - you practise and you practise - and that's what puts you in a position to have intelligent ideas and opinions. Anyone who doesn't like this simple fact can pretend they have some other form of intelligence if they want to, but that won't stop them being stupid - and it won't make them any less of a dipshit either!

## Ignorance

If somebody gives an opinion, ask them why they hold that opinion. Often, it quickly becomes clear that they have never really thought about it and cannot give an intelligent response. It's just what they believe and that's it! They cannot give any rational justification for their opinion because they've never sought to develop one. In such a case, we might say that they are zero degrees away from ignorance. There is no rational thought-process at work - either before they formed their opinion or afterwards.

If they do manage to give some sort of logical and intelligent answer, but when this explanation is questioned, cannot offer a second level of justification, then they may be said to be one degree from ignorance. Even on an issue on which they have actually bothered to form an opinion, their rational defence of their opinion is little more than a facade. It is paper-thin and disintegrates during the very first stage on the most basic level of rational scrutiny.

A slightly more thoughtful person might be 'two degrees from ignorance' - and so on. This is a useful way to sift the amoebas from the semi-humans. More importantly, however, a person's intellectual potential depends upon how they react when their relative ignorance is exposed.

Some people, for example, may be only one or two

steps away from ignorance. However, when it is made clear to them how fragile the foundations of their opinions are, they are, despite their ignorance and shallowness, still willing to learn. They may be willing to change their opinion in the face of an argument they are unable to find flaws in. Perhaps they will at least soften their opinions and withhold judgement on an issue once they realise that they have neglected to think about it in any depth or when the flaws in their arguments are exposed. Or perhaps their failure to rationally defend their opinions will at least encourage them to put a little more effort into exploring issues in the future!

Such people may still be largely ignorant - but at least they have potential. With most people, however, this is not the case. Even if they are several steps away from total ignorance, if they have no inclination to recognise the inadequacies of their arguments and are totally closed to the idea of accepting new ones, if they will not change or soften their opinions even when they cannot justify them, then this casts doubt on their value as a human being.

I remember one particular conversation I had with some shallow bitch who worked as a teacher (A 'Head of Department' no less - and boy did she keep going on about it!).

She was sharing her disgust concerning a fellow teacher who, in the course of speaking to a pupil, had said something she most decidedly disapproved of. "You mustn't call a child an idiot!" she concluded, clearly expecting a sympathetic response and nodding confirmation of her view.

I confess I was impertinent in my response. I simply asked her 'why' you mustn't call a child an idiot. Thanks partly to the limp expression on her face, it quickly became obvious that she'd never actually thought about it before. It had simply never occurred to her that she might ever be required to justify her shallow, thoughtless opinion. She scrabbled for ideas: "It's just totally inappropriate!" she said. "You just can't call a child an idiot."

It's inappropriate? What does that actually mean? It's a trite phrase lacking in any real moral meaning. 'Inappropriate' just means you're wearing a fur coat during a heatwave. No evidence of actual wrongdoing is being offered. Saying something is 'inappropriate' does not constitute an argument as to why the action in question should be considered to be 'wrong' in any way. I explained this to her!

"It's degrading." she said. In response, I suggested that being an idiot was what was really degrading and that if you don't want to be called an idiot, perhaps the best solution is to stop *being* an idiot. Trying to gag everyone else in the world to stop them *calling* you an idiot seems like rather an extreme solution!

"What's an idiot?" I then asked her.

"Someone who does idiotic things," she replied. (This was possibly the most direct and intelligent answer she would ever come to give!)

"So," I asked, "if this child consistently does idiotic things, why shouldn't they be described as an idiot, given that the description is clearly accurate? Even as far as being called an idiot might be degrading, doesn't the use of such a 'degrading' description at least give them an incentive not to be an idiot in the first place?"

She babbled a bit more, took offence at her arguments being dissected and exposed as utter bullshit and then just asked if we could change the conversation. She had begun the conversation as a total idiot. My coaxing dragged her into at least trying to justify her opinions, but - funny thing is - she never thanked me for doing her the inestimable service of exposing her bullshit arguments and giving her the opportunity to amend them. And, despite all her arguments being exposed as vaginal discharge, she never had the courtesy to retract or even qualify her opinion.

But of course such people do not change their ideas either openly or privately. They never say, "Oh yes, you're right! I don't believe that any more because, thanks to you, I can now see my reasoning was deeply flawed." And there's never the slightest hint of gratitude that you've taken the time to show them where they've gone wrong. There's not even a hint that they recognise you were trying to help them - just, basically, resentment. They don't change - they might as well spit in your face - fucking cunts!

# Being Right

One of the most offensive things about being intelligent is that you tend to be right an awful lot of the time. Even when you might not be provably right, no-one has the capacity to clearly demonstrate that you are wrong. You're always ahead of the game, because you have the capacity to think through your opinions and arguments and see for yourself where they might need improving before anyone else does.

Being right nearly all the time annoys the living crap out of people! One of the reasons for this is that many people nowadays seem to believe that there is some sort of United Nations-sanctioned human right that guarantees that they are allowed to be right at least as much as anybody else. No matter how ill-considered, illogical, prejudiced and downright facile their ideas and beliefs are, no-one is allowed to so much as suggest that their ideas and beliefs are any less 'right' or 'valid' than anyone else's.

"It's my opinion," they say, "and I'm entitled to it!" This is true, of course - they are entitled to their opinion (wherever they borrowed it from). This doesn't make them right, of course - the ignorant cunts! It may be their opinion, but they can still be blatantly and obviously wrong and the intelligent person has the annoying ability to be able to prove it.

It is true that there are many issues on which there appears to be no absolute, definitive proof as to what is right and wrong. Annoyingly, for most people, however, the intelligent person is still capable of proving someone wrong simply by applying some basic logic. In most cases, a little questioning and probing, and it becomes clear that the opinion held is often contradictory to various premises or assumptions that the person themselves is not only readily willing to accept, but is actually relying on as part of their own argument. The idiot in question is found to be contradicting themselves.

The uncomfortable fact is that intelligent people have a much greater 'right' than anyone else to be right - or, at least, not obviously wrong - because it is they who have put in the effort to analyse their own opinions, test them using logic and reason and adjust their arguments and opinions for any inaccuracies or inconsistencies that are found. When the discussion or argument arrives, they are simply better-equipped and better-prepared than the other people involved.

I have my own, patented system for ensuring nobody ever wins an argument against me: If someone comes up with a logical, rational point, then I acknowledge and accept it. "That's a good point," I say. I just take on board their logical point and encompass it into my own argument. In this way, no-one can 'win' an argument against me. People 'win' arguments when the other person refuses to accept a point even though it is perfectly rational and obvious.

With my way of doing things, everyone wins, because we can all benefit from having identified rational arguments, regardless of who came up with them. In practice, however, most people are fiercely reluctant to accept criticism or accept their own mistakes and the flaws in their own irrational arguments. Such people 'lose' arguments before they have even begun. They are so incredibly arrogant that, from the outset, they are set against the idea that they might be wrong in any way or that they might have anything at all to learn about anything.

Being right is the result of combining thinking ability with effort, a willingness to learn and a sound sense of principle and morality. We are not all entitled to rightness in equal measure and this really pisses a lot of people off. And yet the intelligent person has done nothing wrong. It is not wrong to think through your opinions and arguments before blurting them out, and just because most people don't do it, doesn't make it wrong! It's not wrong. Hell - never mind wrong - it isn't even illegal! Although it is staggeringly offensive - apparently!

# Semantics

There are some people who, when they have clearly been proven wrong, when you have dissected their arguments and demonstrated them to be irrational and full of holes, have one last, pathetic throw of the dice by saying, "Oh, well if you want to engage in semantics!"

What the fuck? "Yes - I do fucking-well want to engage in semantics, you ignorant fuck, if, by 'semantics,' you mean clarifying what the fuck you are talking about! You want to make out that you're not really wrong - you're only wrong in the sense of your argument not making any sense if one assumes it was being expressed in English rather than in the made-up wankerland language you were actually using, in which 'black' means 'white' and poo refers to some sweet-smelling, fragrant substance! It isn't really a matter of semantics at all - it's just a matter of you being a cunt! That's C. U. N. T.. Cunt! Meaning: Cunt (noun) - Someone like you... you utter cunt!"

# Control

Most people feel distinctly uncomfortable when faced with an intelligent person - and one of the key reasons for their discomfort is the helplessness they feel when they are unable to control someone.

Intelligence requires a distinct capacity to think for yourself. As an intelligent person, your ideas and opinions will have a rational basis built upon sound principles. The opinions of other people will influence you only in so much as they contain well-reasoned, rational thoughts - you are not one to pick up an idea merely because it is popular. Independence of mind, however, is something that makes other people feel most uncomfortable.

The thing is that most people are used to having control over other people. By signalling various degrees of approval or disapproval, they can influence the opinions (voiced and otherwise) and behaviour of those people in their peer group. This sense of control affirms their importance within the peer group. Some members of a group may exert more control than others, but all are reassured that others are, to some extent, seeking their approval in some way. This reassures them about their position and status and helps them to feel comfortable.

Similarly, they show deference to the social group as a whole by allowing others to gain some degree of control over them. By demonstrating their own need to be approved of by other members of their peer group, as well as offering ready approval of others, they, in turn, help others to feel comfortable and feel they have a place within their social grouping. This manipulation and openness to manipulation marks each individual off as a member of the group; of the community of peers. It's all so very, very lovely!

It was also a system used extensively in Nazi Germany. Imagine this pretty little scene from pre-war Germany: "Jews are very nice..." (Signals of disapproval!!) "....er.. .. I mean...nice people ...to murder. Oh yes, and I can show you how good a Nazi I am by showing that I hate Jews even more than you do." And so the conversation continues until strong bonds of friendship and mutual appreciation form. How lovely indeed!

By definition, however, the intelligent, decent person doesn't behave in this way. When he expresses his opinions and ideas, the peer group he is talking amongst start to notice that these opinions are affected not at all by their increasingly desperate and forthright signals of disapproval - or even approval! The intelligent, decent person generally goes right ahead and says what he believes to be right, based on intelligent analysis and moral principles.

People are perplexed by such independently-minded, intelligent people. They cannot understand them. In particular, they have no experience of what it is like to be immune to social pressure.

Quickly following on from this initial perplexity, they get annoyed and upset. It upsets them that they have no means of control over such a person. Furthermore, this person, it seems, is being disrespectful to them by having the temerity to question their bullshit opinions.

As far as the group is concerned, the point of conversation is mutual back-slapping - to try to make each other feel good and to make everyone feel that their views are valued (even when they are not thought through or are merely the products of some selfish bigotry) and that they are all valued and accepted members of the group.

For the intelligent person, a conversation should be a learning experience, enabling each person to learn from the good ideas and criticisms of others - but this sort of thing is, of course, deeply frowned upon in polite society.

You're not playing by the rules! You're not playing to the crowd! You're not open to manipulation! In short; you're not wanted! You're just not enough of a brainless cunt to be acceptable to normal, 'polite' society! Most of all, people will hate you because you are not susceptible to the pathetic social pressures that they meekly enslave themselves to every hour of every day.

# A Threat

If someone shows their intelligence, people don't see it as being helpful - they see it as being a threat!

You wouldn't look at an electrician that way. You wouldn't think, "Oh, he's a very good electrician - but he's a threat! I can't have him coming round and criticising my wiring!" No, you'd think, "Hey, he's a good electrician - that'll come in handy if I'm fixing the house up."

But people don't think; "Hey, this person's really intelligent - that'll come in handy for all sorts of good advice and interesting ideas." No, intelligent people make them feel uncomfortable - or rather, they feel uncomfortable in the presence of intelligent people. They don't like intelligent people. They don't want to learn anything from an intelligent person. They don't want to have a conversation with an intelligent person - or, indeed, suffer the presence of one in their vicinity - and all this despite never openly accepting that anyone more intelligent than themselves even exists.

In some cases, they may have some specific reason to be fearful that a clever person might outmanoeuvre them in some way - get a promotion ahead of them at work perhaps, or outplay them at the poker table. In most cases, however, this isn't what's bothering them. It's your willingness to question people; question their actions, their words, their beliefs - that's what really bothers them.

For most people, the really threatening thing about a clever person is that a clever person might be able to see through their facade and expose their existence as an unprincipled lowlife. This is the real concern behind their hostility - being shown up for what they really are. And, though they may never admit it or openly recognise it, somehow they still know what they are - that's what makes life so painful for them - and they really, really don't like to be reminded of it!

## Character

People don't like to see themselves for what they are, because, in most cases, they are stupid, lazy, shallow, selfish, unprincipled, amoral, prejudice-filled cunts with a sad, desperate desire to be respected, or at least accepted, by the other stupid, lazy, shallow, selfish, unprincipled, amoral, prejudice-filled cunts they surround themselves with.

It is these character traits that prevent people from becoming intelligent in the first place. The reason they don't become intelligent is that they don't practise thinking about anything in any depth - and they don't put the effort into thinking about things, because they simply do not care about being principled and consistent in any way. They don't care about being right - only about whether they get what they want. They cannot think clearly because they cannot or will not free themselves from the constraints of what they want to believe, what it is convenient for them to believe and what it is acceptable for them to believe.

Intelligence is often considered to be some sort of quality that you are born with - perhaps 'enhanced' by education and life's experiences, but, essentially, it is built-in. This isn't really true, however - at least not directly true. What you get

21

born with, if you are to become intelligent, is character. The actual intelligence comes later, after a lot of work.

I've been lucky - I don't delude myself about that. I have worked at my thinking skills, but I was born with the character traits that enabled me to develop them.

Initially, inquisitiveness is key - the desire to learn and the capacity to find joy in discovery. This, however, can easily flounder if you do not have determination. You need the determination to see things through even when there is no joy to be had. You see things through simply because you refuse to be beaten. "To strive, to seek, to find, and not to yield."

Later, developing intelligence becomes a battle against the stupidity you find all around you. You need a certain degree of immunity from the diseased assumptions of the society you live in. Since most people's stupidity is rooted in their desire to conform, it's important to nourish this immunity and nurture it as a source of pride.

For anyone who aspires to be intelligent, there is something to be said for relishing the idea of being a maverick. It helps to have a twinkle in your eye (perhaps even a little glint of evil pleasure) when your perfectly rational argument happens to offend people's sensitivities or goes clean against the accepted and acceptable wisdom of society. It helps to have an instinct towards being disrespectful towards authority, perhaps even towards being thoroughly subversive.

It helps too to instinctively feel just a little uncomfortable about holding any opinion which is too popular - not so much so that it would make you incapable of accepting something simply because it was a commonly-held belief, but seeing that popular opinion is so frequently wrong, it helps to be someone who revels in exploring the alternative possibilities, who revels in thinking what other people dare not even consider.

Most people are not intelligent and they never will be. They do not have the capacity to become intelligent. They do not have the necessary character traits. They do not have 'character.'

You could teach these people thinking skills if only they weren't shallow, lazy fuckwits who don't want to learn. The trouble is; they are! There's no getting away from it. They have neither self-awareness nor the inclination to develop any. They don't see their own flaws - they don't want to see them. Their beliefs are facile nonsense, their arguments are full of shit. They are lazy, of course - they can't be bothered to think about things - but, more than that, they don't want to think about things in case doing so exposes anything about their own characters that they don't want to face up to. Any effort they do put in to thinking is directed, not towards examining their behaviour or beliefs or improving their arguments, but towards deceiving themselves about how full of shit they are. You can try to help them - and I have tried again and again, I still try - but it seems they were born to be cunts!

In such an environment, to remain intelligent, you need fortitude - for when, having become intelligent, you offer your skills to help others, all you get back is hatred and resentment. To be intelligent, you have to get comfortable with that resentment - it has to strengthen you. It can't diminish your resolve - it has to magnify it.

# Arrogance

It really does show what cunts people are when they accuse intelligent people of arrogance. This is not a judgement they make based on any sort of evidence. It is merely a judgement of convenience. They just don't fucking-well like the idea of another person - any other person - being more intelligent than they are. Sometimes, they might grudgingly accept that it is theoretically possible for someone in the world to possess superior intelligence - but they certainly don't like the idea that they might ever actually meet such a person.

If intelligent people really *have* to exist, then they're supposed to exist only in clearly-defined areas. They can be brilliant physicists or mathematicians, but they're not fucking-well supposed to turn up to a social event and point out where fuckwit ordinary people are fucking things up in their shitty, ordinary little lives. Well tough fucking teenage tits! I've got as much right to speak my mind as anyone else - indeed, more so, because I've actually thought about what I say before I open my gob, you fucking, fucking, cunting piece of shit!

No-one normally minds if you take pride in what you do well. You can be proud of being a good pianist, artist or teacher. You can take pride in being a good cleaner. All these things you are allowed to take pride in - but you're not allowed to take pride in being intelligent, because that, apparently, is arrogance.

An exceptionally intelligent person will know from experience that they are not like most other people. They don't pretend to be good at everything, but they know what they are good at.

They know that other people do not think on their level. It would be disingenuous never to admit that this is their honest experience.

Still, most people don't like coming face to face with an openly intelligent person - it makes them feel stupid - which, of course, they are! They don't like facing up to this, however, so they employ a 'coping strategy' which essentially involves being a right cunt and accusing the intelligent person of arrogance.

No, "Oh how wonderful, an intelligent person! How kind of you to offer your skills to help others! Please teach me something so that I can become slightly less of a thick twat than I am now!" - no, just this mean-spirited, spiteful accusation of arrogance. And they do this in total contradiction to what 'arrogance' actually refers to.

Arrogance is an attitude characterised by habitual overestimation of your own abilities and shouldn't really be used to accuse someone who is genuinely brilliant. It is deeply ironic that people make such accusations, since the accusers themselves are often basing their accusations on some absurdly arrogant prejudices and beliefs of their own.

The thing is that you don't get to be intelligent if you are arrogant. Being intelligent requires hard work. Barring some miracle, the intelligent man (or woman) will have necessarily devoted a great many hours to the development of his art. He will have fought and struggled with intellectual matters over many years, honing his skills and building his defences against the temptations of prejudice, selfishness and sloth. He repeatedly tests and examines his beliefs and arguments. When a flaw is found in his reasoning, he corrects it. He is able to adapt and improve his arguments and change his beliefs. This is the very opposite of arrogance.

By definition, he is not arrogant enough to believe that the capacity for intelligence and for intellectual achievement are somehow his by right. The capacity for intelligent thought is a skill, but one that bears testament to diligence and hard work as much as to innate ability.

There is a world of difference between someone who nurtures a delusion that they have some sort of automatic entitlement to rightness unrelated in any way to the amount of effort they put in and someone who thinks they are right because they have carefully studied the issue in question and because they have actually put some hard work into constructing a rational argument.

Arrogance is a characteristic of people who refuse to accept any evidence that they are wrong and thus refuse to change or even adapt their arguments accordingly. If you are the sort of arrogant person who believes they have some sort of god-given right to be intelligent, then you won't learn and you won't get to be intelligent in the first place.

Yet, for many people, it remains an article of faith to refuse to accept that *anyone* they know can possibly be more intelligent than they are - and it is a matter of supreme irony that they will often accuse anyone who suggests otherwise of being arrogant. This is their standard reaction to any suggestion or even hint of superior intelligence from any genuinely intelligent person, even when they know full well that that person is a dedicated thinker. Yet how much more arrogant can you get than assuming that someone who has invested thousands of hours in practising intelligent thinking cannot possibly be more intelligent than you, even though you don't practise at all? Such people refuse to believe that practising intelligent thinking confers any advantages and delude themselves that their own intellectual sloth entails no negative consequences whatsoever!

Cunts! Fucking cunts - that's what they are! I wonder what the collective noun is for cunts, because it would often come in very useful given the hordes - or whatever the collective noun is - of fucking cunts we have everywhere you go these days. Could it be a 'flap'? A flap of cunts? Yes, I think it is! A flap of cunts!

# The Interview

There are few more valuable assets for a business or other organisation than having an intelligent employee in a senior managerial or advisory position - but just try getting a job on the basis of being intelligent! Imagine the interview:

"Why should I give you this job?"

"Because I'm extremely intelligent and can apply this intelligence to doing an effective job."

Where the fuck does the interviewer go from there? If they were more intelligent than you (or even anywhere near as intelligent as you), they might be able to ask questions that would help them to establish whether you really are as intelligent as you claim. However, they are not more intelligent than you and have no capacity to judge or even comprehend your level of intelligence.

To accept your intelligence would be more than they can stomach, so they instantly decide that you are not remotely intelligent at all, but are, in fact, merely arrogant. The basis on which they judge this is that they have decided to believe that it is impossible for you to be more intelligent than they are, and they believe this for no better reason than because they would feel uncomfortable believing anything else... and they would feel uncomfortable because believing you are more intelligent than they are would give them unsatisfactory, though totally justifiable, feelings of inferiority and inadequacy.

Thus you are rejected on the grounds that you are arrogant, a belief based on the absurdly arrogant assumption that you can't possibly be more intelligent than the interviewer.

The interviewer may also hide behind the imaginary rule that 'self-praise is no praise!' This, of course, is nonsense! In job applications and during interviews, self-praise is the name of the game. It is perfectly allowable to highlight your qualifications and experience. You can brag about successful projects you've managed. You can talk up your people skills, your attention to detail and your willingness to work hard. You can hype up out of all reasonable proportion your achievements, negotiating skills, IT skills, marketing skills and so on and so forth ad nauseam. You can make all sorts of outrageous claims of unparalleled dedication to your work. You can blag to the tune of ten times what you are actually worth and no-one seems to mind.

This supposedly general rule about not openly promoting yourself actually only applies to certain specific things. You are allowed to give self-praise in all sorts of ways, but you mustn't make any claim that might be deemed to suggest you are in any way fundamentally more intelligent than anyone else - even though being intelligent is perhaps the most important and valuable business skill of all.

Some interviewers also like to work with the idea that people claiming to be intelligent can't be, because an intelligent person would know that such a claim would lead to them 'failing' the interview. The intelligent person, however, may well not be as desperate to get the job as the interviewer supposes. He may also be testing the potential employer: He will want to know if he might be expected to work with arseholes who get all riled-up and precious over a simple bit of straight-talking. Besides which, he will usually prefer to challenge prejudices rather than pander to them.

It is, in any case, an absurd idea that if you are intelligent, you shouldn't say so, even though it would be the honest answer to a question about why someone should employ you. In practice, however, if your intelligence is the chief reason why you ought to be given the job, then you can either fail to point this out and so be rejected, or you can point it out and be rejected on the basis of supposedly being arrogant. There are, of course, ways around this problem - but, on the whole, they're not very honest ways and why would you want to work for a bunch of cunts anyway?

Of course, you don't actually have to make an open claim to intelligence to provoke such a rejection. You might, for example, be given a problem to solve as a sort of test. When you deliver the solution, the interviewer looks down at the piece of paper so thoughtfully provided for them for the concealment of their personal ignorance, and tells you that your solution, A, is in fact wrong, and that the correct solution is B.

You can either sit there, shut up, and be rejected for the job on the basis of officially getting the answer to the problem wrong, or you can helpfully point out that your solution, A is, in fact, right all along and that official solution B cannot be right thanks to logical point C (a point to which the interviewer has no counter-argument other than to repeatedly insist that this is not what it says on their precious idiot sheet!) and subsequently be rejected on the grounds of arrogance.

You must surely be arrogant since, not only do you think you know better than the interviewer, not only do you think you know better than the person who designed the problem, but, infuriatingly, you are capable of proving it, and willing to do so, possibly in front of other people. Not only this, but, to the great annoyance of the interviewer, you are capable of explaining your proof in a clear, concise and totally rational way, using plain English that even a thick cunt like themselves could understand if they wanted to!

# Propaganda

With so many people around who don't want to accept that any other person they meet might be more intelligent than they are, many convenient myths have developed to enable them to continue this pretence. These myths are supported and promoted by widespread propaganda in popular culture.

In books, films and on television, supposedly 'intelligent' characters usually indicate their intelligence, not by actually being intelligent, but by talking fast or quoting Shakespeare - even though neither habit has anything in particular to do with being intelligent.

They usually work somewhere away from 'normal' people - often in laboratories or with computers - and illustrate their cleverness through their obsession with particle physics, their knowledge of obscure mathematical symbols, or through an uncanny ability to totally reprogramme previously unseen computers in a matter of seconds.

Furthermore, by the laws of social acceptability, these 'intelligent' characters absolutely must have one or more compensatory weaknesses that turn them into idiots. They may be brilliant in their specialist field, but they are no more intelligent in the way they go about everyday life than most ordinary people. Indeed, these 'intelligent' characters are often portrayed as being in some ways dysfunctional in terms of their ordinary lives and when engaged in ordinary activities that other people routinely manage to deal with perfectly well.

These compensatory weaknesses make knowledge of their genius easier for the audience to handle.

Typically, a male scientist will be portrayed as being geeky, shy and not very good with women. This acts as a sop to the audience - he might be brilliant, but he can't get himself a bird, so there's no need for you to be jealous or feel, overall, inferior to him. Therefore, you can go ahead and like him!

Out of such ubiquitous portrayals, the myth arises that genuinely intelligent people only ever display safe skills - usually to do with mathematics, science or computers - that are not likely to make ordinary people feel inadequate or lead to anyone being offended. Furthermore, they won't be able to criticise or ridicule people's real life decisions or dissect their opinions, because they are necessarily totally inept in matters of everyday life and don't understand issues of common concern.

Such myths allow and encourage people to deny that anyone they ever actually meet can possibly be exceptionally intelligent. "You can't be intelligent! If you were intelligent, you wouldn't be here - you'd be far, far away from me; in a laboratory somewhere or working as a university professor! And, in any case, you wouldn't know or understand anything about any issue or subject that affected or interested ordinary people like me!"

This propaganda about intelligent people always being geeky and being essentially dumb in most ordinary areas of life, is essentially born of nastiness. It's similar to wishing that a rich person gets cancer - to 'make up for' their wealth - and make it so that you don't have to be jealous of them!

It's the result of wishful thinking by people who are desperate to find ways (however baseless their criticisms might be) in which they can look down on everyone else. They invent failings which somehow allow them to feel better about themselves. They can only accept someone being clever if they can find another way to look down on them and sneer at them (although, in some communities, someone being clever is itself a reason to sneer at them).

This myth is so pervasive, however, that many people now find it difficult to cope when misleading stereotypes conspicuously fail to fit the facts - so much so that they just make up the facts to fit their prejudices. Faced with an intelligent person with no known compensatory weaknesses, they'll either invent some failings based on nothing but wild speculation or simply refuse to accept that they are intelligent in the first place.

The myth that intelligent people always confine themselves to the lab is, of course, also nonsense. Neither is their genius always confined to highly-specialised and obscure areas of maths, physics or computer science.

In reality, intelligence is not subject-specific. Intelligence does not suddenly cease to function beyond subject boundaries. If a brilliant mathematician or physicist leads an otherwise unintelligent life, then their brilliance is more than likely due to their knowledge and experience or, perhaps, their aptitude with numbers. They may well not be particularly intelligent at all! Knowledge and experience may be subject-specific, but intelligence is not so easily confined.

No - what the genuinely intelligent person really does so effortlessly is make people look and feel stupid! It's not about obscure mathematical theories. It's about picking holes - the big, gaping, logical ones that ought to be obvious - in everything people say and in every opinion and belief they vomit up and then cling so tightly to. His simple questions, even the polite ones, clearly and openly demonstrate people's abject failure to examine to any reasonable degree their own crass behaviour, retarded opinions and unthinking beliefs.

Socrates was, of course, a classic example of the genuine genius. He applied his genius, not to some specialist field of his own, but to the specialist fields of other people. They could choose the battleground - whatever subject they were supposed to be experts in - yet Socrates took only minutes to expose the glaring inadequacies in their views and arguments. This is the genuine genius and genuine intelligence of which people are so terrified. Naturally, they killed him for it!

Genuinely intelligent characters in modern popular culture, however, are vastly outnumbered by those who think they are clever, but are not. Absurd propaganda about intelligent people is even brainwashed into our children. Any character on children's TV that professes or is supposed to be intelligent, routinely turns out clearly not to be. The explanation for their claims of intelligence is pretty much always that they are arrogant and vain. They usually get their comeuppance by being out-thought by someone they look down upon!

It seems society doesn't want to have intelligent people to look up to anymore. We have celebrities instead - and we make celebrities, not out of intelligent or skilled people, but out of drug-taking, facile imbeciles that we can look down upon. Instead of aspiring to be decent and intelligent, people prefer to gawk at celebrities so vain and

stupid they make ordinary unprincipled scum look
good by comparison!

# Judgement

Although I am often falsely accused of arrogance, I
particularly dislike genuinely arrogant people and I
have this marvelous system for sniffing them out. I
simply state very plainly that I am very good at
something - something which I honestly am very
good at and then I watch to see if they scoff, sniff
or turn their noses up at me as if I have said
something appallingly arrogant.
Suppose I say that I am an excellent poker player.
People's immediate reaction, verbal or otherwise,
is to accuse me of arrogance. "Oh really? What the
fuck makes you qualified to judge me - to be able
to make a judgement that I have overestimated
my abilities in playing poker? Have you ever seen
me play poker? Do you even know the rules of
poker? Do you have any fucking clue at all as to
what the game is about or what skills are required
to play it well? You say I'm arrogant, yet you
presume to have some sort of magical ability to
size up people's skills in an area you know fuck all
about! You don't know me. You've never seen me
do the thing I say I'm good at. You have no basis
on which to assess my abilities - yet you go ahead
and accuse me of arrogance. Cunt!"
It's rather amusing, in a way, to see how people's
noses can so easily be put out of joint by such a
harmless and helpful piece of information. Instead
of getting precious, why don't they just ask me to
teach them how to play?
It's also amusing that people sometimes get the
very misleading idea that I'm fishing for respect in

some way. This really does show their poor judgement, because nothing could be further from the truth. I've never needed anyone's respect - except my own. No - all I'm fishing for is a little information. Unlike most people, it seems, I like to have some actual evidence before I accuse anyone of arrogance.

# Criticism

Of course, what is really at the heart of people's stupidity in so many areas is their obsessive, compulsive resistance to accepting criticism, no matter how reasonable, rational, well-meaning and potentially helpful it might be.
In the western world, most people live such a padded, pampered existence that they can blithely reject criticism and carry on being fuckwits, without any immediate threat to their survival. Furthermore, we have such powerful social rules about not hurting people's feelings, that people daren't venture even the mildest criticism of others. And when someone expresses an opinion, the minute you dare to question that opinion, indeed the very second you hesitate to fully endorse that opinion without questioning it, social rules deem that you are being disrespectful.
Such an environment has led many people to become ridiculously and obscenely self-indulgent, arrogant and conceited. They are not used to criticism and can't handle it in a mature and adult fashion. They're so fucking precious that they view even the politest questioning of their thoughtless opinions as being some sort of attack. Their emotional immaturity is such that they are desperate to surround themselves with toadying

friends who are prepared to support their rancid self-delusions - in return for a reciprocal service.

Yet, to shield yourself from criticism is an act of stupidity. Good criticism, no matter how forthright, presents an opportunity to learn. Criticism from an intelligent person can be especially valuable, but people don't even want to know about intelligent people, because accepting someone is exceptionally intelligent involves accepting the implied criticism that they are relatively stupid and that would hurt their feelings. Oh, diddums!

There are those who suggest pandering to such preciousness. "Your criticisms might be more readily accepted," they say, "if you weren't so aggressive," and "if you were more constructive in your criticism."

These people don't seem to realise - or, perhaps, care - that they are proposing 'dealing' with a problem by making it worse. What happens when you pander to people's anti-intellectual prejudices and ridiculous sensitivities is that they get worse. Each time they are not made to face up to their stupidity, they become more conceited and arrogant - and they were usually more than sufficiently conceited and arrogant in the first place. Each time their ludicrous sensitivities are avoided, they expand them or indulge in some new ones.

Besides which, even if you could criticise people without making them feel stupid - where's the fun in that? Rubbing people's faces in their own stupidity is not, in any case, a mere by-product of a quest to get an idea accepted - it is entirely necessary. It is their immature reactions to having their inadequacies shown, that illustrate what the problem is - and, potentially, point to how it can be dealt with.

Don't give me this 'constructive criticism' bullshit! Pandering to a bunch of over-sensitive jerks is just going to make things worse for the next guy who comes along with some well-meaning criticism!

# Consideration

Whilst I'm against pandering to people's ridiculous sensitivities, I have nothing at all against being genuinely considerate and I don't particularly object if people have some basic manners.

When I was young, I don't think that I particularly cared about manners. It was not that I was a rude or disrespectful child - I was generally very polite - but I did not care for the idea that society could dictate how people must behave, right down to the level of some fairly nonsensical, petty rules of social etiquette, or that people would follow these rules out of a need or desire to conform rather than because they were particularly good rules.

I didn't really need to have manners, however, because I had consideration. I was a very considerate child. When my mother gave me 10p once a week to buy some sweets from our village sweetshop, I used to give it back. I liked sweets, as most children do, but I knew my parents weren't rich and, since I ate perfectly well, I would have felt bad spending my parents' money on something I didn't need.

I grew up without too much concern for manners, because I viewed manners as a poor substitute for proper, thoughtful consideration. There are manners and there is consideration. I suppose, however, that manners might sometimes be a useful set of rules for training someone to be considerate if it didn't come naturally to them.

Today, however, our society is churning out school-leavers with no consideration and no manners either. You could have manners without any particular degree of consideration and you can have consideration without any particularly refined manners - but these kids have neither manners nor consideration.

You open a door for them and they just walk straight through without the slightest muttering of thanks. It might not be so bad if they were distracted, trying to be cool or even being deliberately rude, but it's worse than that - they don't even show the slightest hint of appreciating or even realising that something is being done for them.

They don't seem to understand the concept of someone doing anything 'for' someone else rather than for personal gain of some kind. You can imagine them at home. Their "food's on the table!" That's it - the meal is on the table - it has just magically appeared there. They want food! They're entitled to food! There it is!

Of course they know how it got there, but they don't think about or appreciate that something is being done *for* them. "Mum cooks the food. That's what she does. She cooks food because she likes to or because she has to. She wanted to have children, so there's nothing to be grateful for!"

# Gratitude

Many people seem to have a deep reluctance not only to express gratitude, but even to experience it in the first place. They refuse to recognise when someone is doing them a favour or offering to use their skills to help them.

You might occasionally get gratitude if you hold a door open for someone. Perhaps your best chance of a positive response is to bake a cake for somebody - but when you think for someone when they haven't been bothered to think for themselves, when you offer them the benefit of your intelligence, when you point out the flaws in their arguments that they couldn't be bothered to look for and explain how a different way of doing things might actually help them, don't expect gratitude then, because all you'll get is hostility and resentment!

As an intelligent person, highlighting other people's stupidity is your way of trying to help them. A roofer fixes holes in people's roofs. A plumber fixes holes in people's pipes. An intelligent person fixes holes in people's arguments. The intelligent person is being no less helpful than the roofer or plumber - it's just that, instead of being paid for his efforts, he gets resentment.

Any reasonably considerate, polite person would be full of gratitude; "Thank you for pointing out to me the errors of my ways, my inadequacies and my laziness! I apologise for my stupidity and will try not to be such a fuckwit in future!" But, instead, people get all precious and arsy! Ungrateful cunts!

If I offer advice, people might see me as someone who just wants to start an argument or as someone who wants to be listened to or wants to feel important. There's no gratitude there at all! They don't think, "Wow, this is someone who has put in thousands of hours into being so clever! How very kind of this man to offer his advice to me!"

I spend a lot of my time fighting for good causes, pursuing justice and standing up for decent principles. People see what I do. They cannot come up with any rational case as to why I would do such things other than out of kindness - but it almost never occurs to anyone to say a simple "Thank you!"

Nevertheless, I know who I am and what I am here for. This is not a religious viewpoint, as such. It's not about some prophesy in a sacred text. It's just that I understand my nature - I understand the skills I have and what good I can do. If there is a purpose in me being here, then it shouldn't be too difficult to work out what that is likely to be.

# Decency

If you think being intelligent attracts resentment, try being decent as well! That's when the unpleasantness really begins.

I'm an intelligent and decent person. I have a strong moral sense and the staunchness to put my moral principles into action. I try to do what is right rather than merely to serve my own selfish interests. I am not without a sense of mischief, and certainly not immune from error, but my ideas are carefully thought-through and my actions are guided and restrained by my sense of right and wrong. Judging by the reactions I have received throughout my life, however, these are not qualities that are much admired by the public in general. In fact, one could easily get the impression that these qualities are widely despised.

Decency and intelligence combined are a dangerously offensive combination. If you were merely intelligent, you could use that intelligence to deceive people. Having decency, however, may give you tendencies towards being honest. This can have uncomfortable consequences.

When someone is plain wrong about something, you have the intelligence to see that they are wrong and to prove it logically. Without decency, you may decide to keep your points private, to prove your reasoning in silence, to yourself, merely for your own, personal satisfaction. With decency, however, you feel a duty to be honest.

This person, you reason, would be better off if they could learn from their errors and mistakes. Your logic might tell you that they probably won't (and wouldn't want to, anyway), but your decency tells you that you should give them a chance. You don't know for certain that they are an unmitigated arsehole and won't listen to you, and even if you did, you have a duty to give them the opportunity to do so.

They might be a racist, an arrogant pig, a pro-abortion baby-murdering zealot or just plain stupid, and, as a decent person, you have a duty to them and especially to the potential future victims of their stupidity to give them a chance to see the errors of their ways.

So, with the burden of duty resting heavily on your shoulders, you tell them what a stupid, ignorant cunt they are and how they should change their ways. An uncomfortable atmosphere unreasonably descends! They tell you to fuck off. They might argue with you first. You dutifully, kindly and rationally point out the logical and rather embarrassingly large holes in their arguments. Then they tell you to fuck off!

Being a decent person, you may either accept it with good grace, or, alternatively, follow them down a dark alley and mercifully - and with the well-being of mankind in your thoughts - brutally batter them to death. Either way, you haven't made any new friends - although, in the later case, a certain amount of smug satisfaction may compensate!

Being intelligent and decent is certainly not the route to popularity. Fortunately, intelligence and decency give you the sort of confidence and self-assurance that no degree of popularity can ever provide!

# Resentment

It is wonderful to be intelligent. You get to enjoy the benefits of having made so many intelligent decisions. And life has so many interesting things for you to think about and consider. Living an intelligent life, however, means you notice the ignorance, stupidity, selfishness and conformity in the world - and you see it first hand, every day, in the way other people treat you.

If you are intelligent, principled, decent and honest, then life is an experience of being treated with suspicion and as a threat. The suspicion is prompted by your kindness. People wonder what it is you want - as if your kindness is nothing more than an underhand ploy. People despise you. Your thoughts and ideas are nothing but grasps for attention! Your analysis is a condescending assertion of your superiority! Your advice is a sign of arrogance and conceit - why else would you think you know better than anyone else about anything?

I wasn't born with or brought up to have any particular artistic talent, but I don't resent people who were. I don't resent musicians because they are more musical than me. Living an intelligent life, however, is an experience of being treated with constant resentment. People resent your very existence.

It is not in my nature to feel sorry for myself. Indeed, I revel every day in being the argumentative, insensitive old git who continually upsets and offends people by committing the appalling crimes of saying what he thinks and standing on principle - "just to be awkward," apparently! That doesn't change the fact that people shouldn't be treated this way. It isn't right.

## Actions and Manner

The intelligent way to judge a person is by their actions and by their decisions. You only really see what a person is like when they are faced with a choice between what they know to be right and the expedient alternative that they believe better serves their own selfish interests. That's when you can discover their character, their motivations, their priorities and their true values. That's when we really get hard evidence of what they are made of and of what sort of person they really are.

When a person offers you their support, even though it does not seem to be in their interests, that's when we can finally be confident of their humanity. Much more frequently, when a person stabs you in the back for financial gain or in order to preserve their own popularity, that's when you can safely confirm what a shitty little arsewipe they are.

Your work colleagues may be perfectly pleasant and nice to you. In many cases, however, that's just because they can't be bothered with the hassle that would result if they told you what they really think of you.

In everyday, cosy situations when selfish interests happen to coincide with apparently decent behaviour, it can be hard to tell for sure what people are really like. In the absence of hard evidence from people's actual actions and decisions, we may sometimes have to rely more on less substantial evidence; what people say, their general 'manner' and so on. Many people, however, become so used to and so obsessed with routinely judging people by their words or manner, that they actually ignore the far more solid evidence provided by people's actions.

I remember one woman I used to work with who was planning on going on a sponsored walk (of only a few miles) for charity. She left her sponsorship form in a prominent place at work whilst she took time off work to go and fly off on yet another of a series of extravagant holidays abroad.

It's fine that she did a sponsored walk - and perhaps got a few quid out of people who would otherwise be too tight to contribute to charity - but she never showed willing to make any sort of meaningful sacrifice in terms of what she spent on herself. If she'd have given up her holiday, she'd have raised many times what her sponsored walk achieved. Didn't the sponsored walk mainly just help her to gloss over her own rather excessive and extravagant entertainment budget?

She talked a good game about her favourite charity - but it's her actions, not her words, that reveal her real attitude. Most people, however, insist on being blind to such obvious truths. So long as it suits them to do so, they'll quite happily take the words at face value, even though these may contradict the actual decisions that have been made by the person in question.

Talk is cheap. It is easy for a person to say they have values, but we only find out what their true values are when they are asked to make a sacrifice on behalf of someone other than themselves. That's when we find out what they really care about.

"You're my brother - and family always come first!"
"Really? Can I borrow some money then?"

"Oh, I don't know! Money's a bit short at the moment! My money's all tied up! I've got a bit of a cash-flow problem myself!"

How many people have brothers like that? How many people are like that? Mankind, on the whole, is a shitty, slimy disgrace of a species. Principled people are the rare exception to the rule.

As a principled person, I put a lot of time and effort into being a decent and kind person, but virtually no time or effort whatsoever into presenting myself as a decent and kind person. I may even be provocative in what I say and in the way I say it. I know that my actions ought to be the things by which I am judged and it helps me assess the character of other people by seeing whether they respond to my actions or to some ludicrous, unscientific and prejudicial misinterpretation of my manner. It is not just a case of seeing whether they are capable of making judgements based on a person's actions rather than their manner - it is also about seeing whether they are even interested in doing so.

Many people are simply not remotely interested in what you are. They are not interested in your qualities as a person - they are not interested in kindness or intelligence. They are far more interested in how you present yourself. If you don't put up an acceptable facade, you are not likely to be well thought-of. If being associated with you will not help them in their desperate climb up the status ladder, then why would they want to know you at all?

Whatever faults I may have, the facts of my actions repeatedly demonstrate my willingness to put principle above my own selfish interests. How much of the money I earn, for example, do I spend

47

on myself - on alcohol or things for my own entertainment? Hardly anything! Partly I'm lucky in that the things I consider entertaining don't happen to cost very much - but mainly I restrict my spending because I can't morally justify frivolously and selfishly lavishing the world's valuable resources on myself when I am already so well-off. My spending is not held back by what I can afford - but by what I can morally justify. This doesn't make me a saint - it just makes me different from most of the greedy, selfish bastards you see in the street every day who choose hardly ever to consider anything in life other than what they want for themselves.

I'm generous with my time and efforts and eager to offer what skills I have when I think they might be useful to other people. People ought to be able to see from my actions that I am principled and kind and regard my manner to be of lesser importance - but, instead, their discomfort with my 'disrespectful' questioning and my forthright manner is allowed to override the proof given by my actions!

Judging people by their words or manner may be useful when you haven't seen their actions; their actual decisions between moral and immoral alternatives - but to judge someone by their words alone in complete contradiction to their known actions is ridiculous and obscene!

# Values and Principles

Some people - though progressively few - can give what might initially appear to be principled justifications for many of their actions, decisions and beliefs. Question them further, however, and, in almost all cases, it quickly becomes apparent that some of their decisions seem to be severely at odds with some of their other decisions. Specifically, their justifications for some decisions leave them unable to justify some of their other decisions without blatantly contradicting themselves.

Try asking someone; "Do you think gay teachers should be allowed to teach in schools?"

"Yes - of course! Everyone should have a right to a private life. What people get up to outside of work should be their own business. It's got nothing whatsoever to do with their employer. No-one should be refused a job on the basic of their sexuality. A person's sexual orientation is their own private business!"

"So, do you think paedophiles should be allowed in teaching?"

"No - of course not!"

"Hang on! You just said, 'No-one should be refused a job on the basic of their sexuality!'"

"Yeah - but...but....but....."

As in this example, most people do not base their decisions and opinions on clear principles and values. What they actually do is make an instinctive judgement on individual issues, often based on what they feel would be socially-acceptable, and then attempt to come up with a rational-sounding justification for their decision or belief.

The person in this particular example knows she's not supposed to say anything negative about gay people. She knows society demands that she supports gays in teaching. She comes up with a barrage of 'principles' to justify her stance, but the paedophile question clearly demonstrates that she doesn't believe in a single one of them!

Of course a criminal paedophile could be barred from schools, but that's not because of their sexual orientation - it's because they've shown themselves willing to abuse children. A paedophile who resists his urges ought to be admired. Yet, in this example, the woman in question is seeking to bar someone from teaching, purely on the basis of their sexual orientation, without the slightest evidence of any actual wrongdoing and in total contradiction to her stated principles.

Most people, it seems, have no desire to base their decisions or beliefs on a decent and consistent set of principles and values. They don't really understand what it means to have principles or values. They invent 'principles' to justify whatever beliefs and opinions they happen to find convenient, rather than make decisions based on any sort of principles.

No matter how rational their justifications sound, their thinking process is not rational, because their justification is merely an afterthought - it stems from their desperate attempts to justify their ad-hoc decision or belief. It's like voting for a politician because you like their hairstyle and then attempting to justify your choice by waffling incoherently about their economic policies!

Intelligent people have taken the time to think about what their basic values and principles are - and they base their decisions and opinions upon the coherent set of values and principles that they have developed.

If, on the other hand, you justify one decision by reference to a particular set of values, then justify another decision by reference to a completely contradictory set of values, as most people do, then all that really tells us is that you probably don't have any values - at least none that you've actually thought about - or that you're a gutless, arrogant liar who'll say anything to retrospectively justify your unprincipled, selfish and expedient words and actions.

# Decisions

Mankind is a rational species, people suppose. The truth, however, is that rational decision-makers are rare and exceptional individuals in a vast colony of unimaginative conformists. Mankind, as a species, consists primarily of fuckwits no more capable of rational decision-making than most animals - in many ways, even less so, because the animals' survival instincts preserve some sort of rationality that many humans have lost. Humans who don't have to worry about survival frequently choose to ignore rationality. Their lives are an indulgence of surplus over reason.

Most people appear to make decisions, but they do so with almost total disregard for any sort of rational process. They often fail even to consider what options are available - an outcome is reached, but no decision as such has really been made as no alternatives were actually considered. They fail to ask themselves what constitutes a 'good decision' or a 'successful' outcome. They don't consider things logically, weigh up options, consider the pros and cons and then make a decision. A decision is made - and then superficially rational-sounding points are foraged for and added on as belated justifications.

The decision-making few, the genuine thinkers, the rational elite - these are just the few amongst the many, amongst the multitude of worker ants guided by little more than vague, selfish instincts and a deformity of the mind that makes them desperate to conform to the norms of our depraved society. Mankind is a species of fuckwits. The odd exception does not a fucking summer make!

# Old Age

I have good reason to think that, especially in years gone by, my discourses with young people have sometimes had a profound effect. Some of them even seemed to experience something of an enlightenment - and they seemed to relish the prospect of the new world that had been opened up for them. I don't know if the effect ever lasted.

Older people, even those barely in their twenties, may have discussions, but when, if ever, is there any sign that the discussions you have with them affect their behaviour in any way? Even when they are capable of discussing a new idea intelligently - and very few are - they no longer seem to have the capacity to follow a new idea to the point of allowing it to affect their actual decisions. They've reached an age when the decisions they make are taken according to their experience, the way they've seen things done before and the way they've done things before.

In many ways, they are ready for the grave, ready for death because they cannot change, they cannot take on board new ideas. They are just winding round on a routine that takes them towards death.

And the age at which this is happening seems to be getting younger and younger - you now get seventeen-year-olds, sixteen-year-olds, fifteen-year-olds who have already closed their minds to new ideas. Teenagers already so old and inflexible, so close-minded that they are incapable of making a positive contribution to society! They're old in the head and consequently ugly as hell!

# Conversation

I never really grew up to be much of a conversationalist - or, at least, that's what I used to think. I was fine to talk about something of substance - I could happily discuss current affairs or philosophy - I just didn't 'chat'. Now I realise it's not me who is not much good at conversation - it's all those cunts who make up most of the rest of the world!

I'm actually very good at conversation, it seems. I have something to say, opinions and ideas to offer and I'm open, willing and keen to learn from other people - the trouble is that they don't have anything remotely life-enhancing to say.

It used to be old women who did 'chit-chat.' A man, after a pointless conversation with a third party, might have turned to his friend and sarcastically asked, "Well, what did we learn from that?" - implying that conversations normally had a point, only this one had been unusually pointless. Now, everyone seems to be into pointless wittering.

A great deal of conversation now seems to consist of little more than a simplistic reporting of what people did or what they said (usually along the lines of, "I went .... and she goes ......"). Why so simple, so barren, so safe and so fucking boring?

People are no longer expected to be prepared to ask or answer any questions about what they actually *think* about anything. To ask such a question of someone is to expect them to have an opinion, to have thought about something - and that could be awkward and embarrassing. And to answer such a question would risk causing offence. How awkward it would be if they didn't all share the same sad-arsed, socially-acceptable opinion!

Politically-correct rules about what you can and cannot say make people so tentative about directly discussing anyone's actual opinions at all. People generally only volunteer an opinion when they feel sure it will be accepted without question or argument. No-one in the conversation has any expectation that their own views will be challenged, or any intention of challenging anyone else's opinions.

This is a reflection of a deeply oppressed society that has been taught to despise independent, intellectual thinking. The only type of thinking allowed is thinking that only ever comes up with socially-acceptable opinions - but that is no type of thinking at all!

Even in our schools, children are no longer asked to ever form or explain their own, individual opinions. The schools don't want to risk anyone saying anything 'unacceptable' or 'offensive.' The bastards who run our education system don't care about children developing thoughtful opinions. They're only interested in children learning and abiding by what is 'acceptable' and 'unacceptable.'

A child's progress should be judged by how much they've thought about their opinions and whether they can justify them. They shouldn't be judged by what their opinions are - that's where brainwashing starts! Independent thinking is seen as highly subversive, so children's independent thinking skills are deliberately repressed. Our schools seem to be seeking to turn children into vegetables - and, in most cases, they succeed.

No wonder young adults don't have anything to say for themselves! After such an oppressive childhood, they've become conditioned not to openly invite or discuss opinions during a conversation. They're trained to avoid anything that might be awkward or challenging in any way.

People no longer abide by the notion that you should be able to take something away from a conversation - a new idea, a new piece of knowledge or even just a new joke. Not only do they not really expect to learn anything - they have nothing to give during the conversation either. Selfish cunts!

Most conversations, it seems, are for little more than mutual backslapping. They provide the comfort of a human voice, the comfort of simply being in conversation, regardless of how facile the conversation is. Nothing worthwhile is being said, nothing is being learnt, no-one's understanding is being advanced and no real friendship is being developed.

A conversation is just an indulgence in superficiality and selfishness. People want someone to sit there, nod at them, agree with everything they say and totally refrain from challenging them in any way. They are so fundamentally insecure that they seek only to hear things which make them feel good about themselves. If the person they have the conversation with doesn't make them feel good, then they don't want to have the conversation - it's me, me, me, selfish, selfish, selfish the whole time! They don't want to learn and they have nothing to offer during the conversation except a reciprocal arse-licking service - the boring cunts!

# Reassurance

To get them safely through to the grave, young people especially seem to seek and need almost constant reassurance - reassurance of their place, reassurance of their importance to other people, or even just reassurance that other people continue to be aware of their existence (regardless of how pointless their existence is!).

Other than through inane conversations, they get this superficial reassurance through their addictions to text-messaging, 'social-networking' and the like. Through such media, they seek a nirvana of constant reassurance - they do not want to have to cope with the dire consequences of going a single minute without someone posting them a message or acknowledging their existence in some way.

They can't be bothered to actually do anything or help anyone so that they actually are important - that would involve too much effort. Instead they seek to replicate the thrill of actually being important by simply having people tell them they are important - or, at least, indicate their importance by responding, however superficially, to their texts, posts and other messages. The depth and quality of communication that might bring more meaningful happiness is inadequately replaced by sheer quantity and constancy of superficial pap!

These young people are, of course, suffering from a debilitating addiction. Their obsessive behaviour in constantly checking for 'updates' is also a symptom of their desperate lack of self-esteem. They have little, if anything, by way of a sense of self-worth, other than that which relies, rather tragically and precariously, on constant but inane reassurances from other pointless little pricks.

A gunman goes on a rampage on a Norwegian island. A bunch of adolescents are shot dead - but so what? Frankly, I find it difficult to care - not because they were Norwegian Labour Party supporters, but because I find it difficult to imagine a modern teenager who isn't a waste of space and a waste of oxygen, fucking-well obsessed with text messages and social networking, sending and receiving endless facile messages at all times of day and night and never having the slightest worthwhile thing to say or write.

The chances of any of the 'victims' not being a total fuckwit was - let's face it - embarrassingly low! Even when they know there's an insane gunman on the loose, all they can think of to do is to start texting people - again and again! Their mobile phone is their 'comfort blanket.'

Nevertheless, I don't approve of shootings like that. It's thoroughly unintelligent to even take a chance on people's guilt or innocence when it isn't exactly difficult to find some fuck against whom there is clear evidence on an individual basis. There's plenty of bang-to-rights, proven cunts queuing up to be killed. Executing these motherfuckers shouldn't be some speculative punt.

# Distraction

Besides providing short-lived reassurance, mobile phones, texting and social networking are relatively new additions to mankind's extensive list of distractions.

Some say that people fill their time with meaningless nonsense in order to distract themselves from thinking about death. Perhaps more commonly, people are trying to distract themselves from thinking about life. Modern economies seem actually to revolve around people's desire to distract themselves from thinking about values or principles or facing up to the important tasks and difficult decisions in life.

People work long hours and spend much of the rest of the time dousing their brains in alcohol or vegetating in front of the telly or pointlessly poxying about on the internet or mindlessly fiddling with their mobile phones - all this to give them 'something to do.'

People seem to be scared of the prospect of having thinking time and need distractions to help them avoid facing up to anything of genuine important. They're even so scared of the prospect of bringing up children that they prefer to be distracted by the desire to earn money, so that other people, the games console and the internet can bring their children up for them! Is the pursuit of profit and financial gain simply the most effective distraction we have ever invented?

Along with shopping, of course! The things people buy - do they buy them because they need them or is the shopping and selection process merely a distraction and therefore an end in itself?

And then there's eating! Of course it is important

to eat - but not that much! Many people's lives, however, stutter along from one meal or sugary snack to the next one. "What shall I eat next?" becomes a constant distraction. Is that the real source of the obesity epidemic?

In many ways, our western society lives in poverty - and this is hopefully how it will be seen by future generations and cultures. The internet, mobile phones, texting and social networking - aren't these, for most people, just effective ways of wasting time - a modern way of filling the void? Is life to be no more than a distraction between birth and death?

More and more people appear to seek nothing but to distract themselves from their slow march towards the grave. In many cases, it would seem a kindness to ease their burden somewhat and shorten the time that they have to kill.

The desperation to distract ourselves is highlighted when you have scientific endeavours reported in the news. When you have news reports about space travel, expeditions, laboratory experiments and the like, journalists say such things as, "Yes, but what's the point? Why should we spend money on these things? What practical applications does it have?"

The scientists are expected and tempted to go along with this and say, "Oh, well this could bring enormous dividends to ordinary people's lives. Something developed for the space race could have practical applications in your kitchen - the non-stick frying pan is an example!"

What are you doing? Don't play their game! Just turn around and say, "What sort of a fucking philistine are you? It's there to be discovered, let's go and discover it! It's there to be explored, let's explore it! Not everything has to come down to whether it has a practical application in your kitchen, you fucking twat!"

Besides which, the whole argument is arse about tit! It isn't that the space race is there to help ordinary people in their kitchens - it is that ordinary people and their kitchens are there so that they can do the menial tasks that enable other people to go and explore space and unlock the secrets of the universe on behalf of mankind.

These silly questions from journalists reflect an annoyance amongst the population that they are being distracted from their petty, meaningless existences and are being asked to pay attention to - and even actually pay for - mankind's quest to discover new things and learn about the universe we live in. People are annoyed because they see scientific discoveries as expensive and irritating distractions from the really important business of shopping, eating and texting. Fuckwits!

# The Lifeless and the Dead

I have a little part-time job that gets me out into the fresh air - I make deliveries - and, as part of this job, I see a lot of shop assistants. On weekends or after school hours, it's quite common for these small shops to employ girls around or about seventeen years old. Perhaps the shop owner likes to employ what he sees as 'young totty' to 'keep the customers happy!' Perhaps it's because he doesn't have to pay them the full minimum wage. Probably it's just the sort of job that seventeen-year-old girls tend to apply for - the sort of job their mothers consider 'suitable' for a girl that age trying to earn some pocket money.

A lot of these kids, like most people their age, are so fucking rude! I don't mean because they swear at you or anything like that - they're just such non-entitites, such pleasantry-free zones with nothing to say for themselves. I try smiling, saying hello, telling a joke, enquiring after their interests, making what ought to be thought-provoking observations - but nothing of any substance ever comes back.

They're usually still at school, but they have no interest even in the things they have chosen to study. They may, for example, study science, but they have no interest in any sort of scientific discoveries. Invariably, they have not the faintest idea what science is - they're only interested in passing an exam and receiving a piece of paper.

Most of them have nothing whatsoever to offer, not even smalltalk. You might get a bleary, grunted hello out of them if you say hello to them first, but the idea that they might ever say something even as simple as, "And how are you

62

today?" - it's beyond them!

They never start a conversation themselves, never ask a question, never offer an idea or a snippet of news or make a polite enquiry - nothing - just lifeless wastes of space. Most of the time they just want to stare blankly into their mobile phones, desperately searching for a new text message - a facile snippet from facile friends to say they haven't been forgotten - whilst taking no interest in the world in general or in what's happening in their immediate vicinity.

Some look thoroughly miserable. Some put on painfully superficial half-smiles with not the slightest hint of personality or warmth behind them. They might briefly smile or laugh if you say something pleasant or amusing, but they appear totally unable to set off a cheery mood or show any sort of initiative. There have always been shy teenagers - but this is beyond that - it's utter lifelessness!

I don't like to see young people wasting their lives and letting their brains turn to mush, so I'm always on the look out for signs that a young person might want to open up some new horizons.

There was one shop girl I spoke to regularly on my rounds. She didn't seem nearly as miserable as most. She'd shown a flicker of interest in one or two things I'd said. She claimed to have an interest in being educated - she was studying hard, apparently! She didn't seem to have much to say for herself - but I like to give people the benefit of the doubt.

As a nice little gesture, I drove round one evening, to the shop where she worked, and offered to lend her a book of mine which I thought she might benefit from reading. And when I say a book of mine, I don't just mean one I had bought; I mean a book I had written.

"Wow!" She didn't know I'd written a book. "Nice!" She was, however, too busy, she said, what with studying for exams and so on, to have time to read my book. That's right - too busy being 'educated,' too busy chasing meaningless certificates to have time to read a book - and not a very long one at that!

Well, OK, fair enough! A poor decision, I thought, but one she is entitled to make. I offer help, it's not accepted - but no big deal! Just another brainless decision from someone who is not very good at sizing up an opportunity. Just the normal sort of brainlessness you might expect from anyone.

But there was more! She never even said "Thank you!" - no "Thank you" that the offer had been made or for me having dropped in especially to offer her my help on nothing but the off-chance that she might be bright enough to make use of it. And just forget about appreciating that I'd spent years writing the book!

And this was not just a momentary lapse - she never, ever said "thank you." OK, so she was too short-sighted to make use of it - but she was also so pig ignorant and inconsiderate that she never stopped to realise that someone was being kind to her, trying to do her a favour. She probably wonders why I hardly ever bother speaking to her any more.

Perhaps she was suspicious of my motivation - but I don't care; she certainly had no good reason to be suspicious. I'm not responsible for her fucking prejudices! Fucking ungrateful cunt!

There was another girl I met on my rounds who did

initially seem to have a little bit of life in her. She was a little shy, but she had a pleasant enough smile and perhaps even a little sense of mischief.

I told her a little about my expertise in certain areas. I said what a pity it was that so many young people her age were only interested in passing exams and accumulating certificates rather than in actually being educated. I asked if she was interested in being educated and she said she was. She readily agreed that we should meet up some time, away from work, and I could explain how I might be able to help her. A time and place was arranged.

So far, so good - an honest and straightforward offer of help from a 'wise old man' (if mid-thirties is 'old') to a young person apparently eager to learn. However, she e-mailed and then phoned to cancel our arrangement. She was most apologetic. Her mother, it seems, was most unhappy. She was 'going all weird' - behaving most peculiarly - and would not allow her daughter to keep her appointment.

As far as the mother was concerned, it seems, the only reason a man of my age would so much as talk to a seventeen-year-old girl was in order to trick her into practising the most depraved sexual acts known to mankind. It couldn't possibly be anything else!

To her, the occasional sensational story in the snootier parts of the tabloid press was the whole world - and justified her, not just in suspecting the worst, but in actually treating a person against whom she knew nothing other than entirely positive things, as if he were a sick pervert intent upon abusing her daughter.

To have made a few discreet enquiries would have

been one thing. To have privately suggested to her daughter that they should first meet in a public place - an understandable, if somewhat paranoid, precaution. (To have invited this man round for tea would have been the classy, old-fashioned way to get an opportunity to size him up and calm her own irrational fears.) In fact, she felt absolutely no shame at all in openly treating that man with utter contempt without the slightest evidence to back up her suspicions or the slightest recognition that she even might be wrong about him.

No doubt if her daughter had made the same arrangement with a female or with a young lad her own age, there would have been no objections. If I had been black, she might have been more hesitant about displaying her prejudices. As it was, she showed no shame at all. What a bitch! I'd like to shove that cow's head into a fucking wood pulper! "What did you say, you fucking bitch? What did you say? Sorry, I can't hear you over the noise!"

I made some further, polite enquiries to see if there was anything I could do to soothe the mother's concerns. My background, I noted, was in the security services and in teaching. There was hardly likely to be anyone in the entire country her daughter would be safer with. Her prejudices, however, remained firmly intact.

At first, the seventeen-year-old tried to shrug off her mother's rather unclassy attitude as just the knee-jerk reaction of an overprotective parent - but then, it seems, she did some rather cold (if misguided, as it turns out) calculations about where her bread was buttered. Pissing off her mother - despite the old cow obviously being in the wrong - would cause her more hassle, more 'agro' than being a bitch to a kind man she saw only occasionally at work and even then only briefly. So what she did do?

One might have thought she could at least have managed a simple e-mail, saying; "I'm terribly sorry, but things are awkward for me and I shall not be able to correspond with you for the foreseeable future. Nevertheless, I would like to thank you for being ever so kind to me and I wish you all the best. I am sorry for any inconvenience I have caused you."

What she actually wrote, in response to a most considerate enquiry, was; "Don't contact me again. I'm not interested in you. Delete my contact details and leave me alone." Now, what the fuck possesses a person to treat someone like that? It could be a very dangerous thing to do - I'm tempted to make sure of it!

Fucking bitch! Still, that's how a young life is crushed - through such simple means. It's sad when young people are crushed like that. They're not in a war zone, they're not threatened with destitution, but, somehow, they feel so much social pressure that it saps the will and life right out of them. They become gutless, pathetic, empty shells - they've crossed the line and sold their souls to live a boring, unimaginative, unintelligent life of miserable conformity. The choice has been made.

This particular girl has now taken to wearing such a scowl that it has had a permanent effect on her features. She no longer has the capacity to form a nice smile. Her face now is gnarled and ugly. And that's the pretty side compared to what is going on inside. Barring a miracle, she's finished...and at just seventeen years old! What sort of a cunting bitch of a mother would do that to her own

67

daughter? She goes on my list - there's no doubt about that.

# Ruined

For much of history, seventeen would have been considered an ideal age for a bride. She'd be in the full bloom of youthful womanhood and at the peak of her natural fertility, but she'd be sufficiently mature to take on the responsibilities of motherhood. The perfect companion and a prize catch for an alpha male!

These days, however, so many young women - by the age of, say, seventeen - are basically already ruined in terms of both their sexual and general attractiveness. They're already too fat, too stupid, too conceited, too arrogant, too prejudiced, too politically-correct, too brainwashed and too shallow to be considered remotely attractive by any reasonably discerning male. They are already ruined in terms of their physique, their intellect and their character.

I'm not expecting perfection. The prettiest girls aren't always the brightest and the kindest ones aren't always the prettiest. A little extra weight might be OK if there's some extra personality to go with it. The vast majority of seventeen-year-olds, however, seem to have almost nothing at all to offer a man except their willingness to get drunk and 'get laid'!

Take a hundred seventeen-year-old girls from this country at random. The vast majority are in an appalling physical condition. It's not just that they aren't particularly toned - many of them are fat and an obscene proportion are already obese. Many have already developed the sort of grotesque

68

body shape that could put you right off your food just by looking at it. Shame it doesn't put them off theirs!

Even those who are not fat tend to be extremely unfit. They can't stretch, move or run anywhere near as well as people from previous generations - even now!

Even the thin ones are generally only thin because they starve themselves and not because they participate in any sort of significant exercise. Of the few that do regularly participate in sport, most of them still look desperately heavy-footed and lacking in any sort of grace or lightness in the way they move.

And then, after you've eliminated the physically unfit girls, look at the ones you have left! Look at the ugly scowls on their faces! These scowls are not the expression of some temporary fit of disapproval. These are physically-ingrained scowls brought on by almost constant mardiness. These long-term scowls reflect a selfish, uncultured, uneducated, close-minded attitude towards life in general and anything intellectually challenging in particular. Call me fussy, but I like a girl with an attractive smile - and this isn't something that's easy to fake.

And if you've still got any of the original one hundred left, listen to them - listen to their loud, raucous, uncultured voices! Most don't even know how to sound feminine or demure. And if you have any left then, do any of them have any brains - any interesting things to say, any reasonably well-considered opinions? Can any of them leave their mobile phone alone for more than five minutes other than when they are asleep?

I reckon that if you find one in a hundred that you

can genuinely say is physically fit, has a nice smile, a pleasant, feminine manner and has something intelligent and interesting to say for herself, then you can count yourself lucky in this day and age.

And they're only going to get worse! They eat and they drink and they eat and they sleep around and they eat and they vegetate in front of the television and they eat - and all whilst constantly fiddling on their mobile phones.

They wait until they're fat and in their mid-thirties before they even consider getting married or settling down with a man. They're getting married when they're already twice the natural age for starting a family. Why would any discerning male pick a brainless, overweight hag who's already reached what would have been a generous life expectancy throughout much of history? He'd have to be pretty desperate!

# Charity

Most young people are constantly oppressed by idiots - by their peer group and, often, by their parents too. Now even their teachers take part in this appalling betrayal of everything a teacher ought to stand for. But what if these young people had the chance to be free?

There can be few more valuable opportunities for a young person than getting the opportunity to meet, talk or work with a genius; a genuine intellectual, a free thinker. I am a genius. I am extraordinarily intelligent. It makes sense that I should use my skills to help others.

In my time, I've taught in many schools and volunteered with a number of youth organisations. I've always been good with kids and teenagers. Even many adults who themselves found my manner disconcerting and who disapproved of my subversive approach, sometimes could not help but admit that I sometimes managed to awaken a special fascination within young minds. They could sense I had some sort of special talent, even though they may not have understood what it was.

I used to do a lot of good with young people. I nurtured their inquisitiveness, their thirst for discovery. I opened up new possibilities for them not to conform. I showed them another way to live a life, albeit a way they had never previously missed, because they had never known about it. I showed them independence and I showed them freedom. I showed them mischief.

These days, however, there is a very widespread and oppressive movement that seeks to stop this sort of thing happening. Young people, it seems, are at risk from people like me who might seek to

71

do horrible and depraved things to them - specifically, I might undermine their desire or need to conform. Obviously, encouraging young people to use their minds and think for themselves - well, it's an appalling act of desecration and young people must be saved from such sickening perversity!

I still volunteer to help young people. Over recent years, however, nearly all of my enquiries with schools or youth organisations seem to stir up the most absurd degree of totally unjustifiable, paranoid hostility from the very people whose job it is to look after the interests of the young people in their charge.

Just try contacting a school to offer your help in any sort of intellectual way! Witness the immediate aura of suspicion with which you get treated and the pitiful ways in which they try to fob you off! It's utterly sickening. Our society seems intent upon systematically cutting off each generation of school children from society - so they can be brainwashed without interference.

Not so long ago, I tried to volunteer my talents to a well-known youth organisation for girls. Their website made it absolutely clear that they were desperate for volunteers - male as well as female, they said. They had tens of thousands of girls whose membership applications they could not accept because they didn't have enough volunteers.

I'd worked mainly with boys' organisations in the past, but, through teaching, I'd had lots of experience with teenage girls too. I was ready to help out if I could. Yet, when I made initial enquiries about volunteering, the air of suspicion and hostility in their regional office was apparent from the start and grew rapidly from there. A bloke volunteering in a girls' organisation? You could hear their paranoid alarm bells ringing from almost a hundred miles away.

Their mission statement said they sought to help girls develop their intellectual abilities and to develop their independent thinking skills. I e-mailed them and suggested that this was my area of expertise and that my particular skills - my intelligence, my independence of mind - would come in very useful, especially for their older girls in their sixteen-plus section.

Obviously my e-mail caused some considerable confusion. Indulgent, as they were, in a number of absurd prejudices, they seemed unable or unwilling to grasp what it was I was offering to help with.

Having asked for and received further explanations, the stuck-up cunts seemed to be deeply offended that I was suggesting I might have intellectual skills that their other volunteers did not have. They took umbrage and snootily refused to answer any of my perfectly reasonable questions. They refused even to give me a contact number or even a name for a local representative with whom I might be able to discuss matters further.

Communication was difficult at the best of times. Perhaps as a result of their texting addictions, they seemed unable to understand simple English or to write in coherent sentences. It's so fucking rude when people can't be bothered to construct complete sentences. They don't bother to check what they have written. They thoughtlessly jumble words together and assume that the reader will be able to get the general gist of what they want to say. And these were not part-time volunteers

73

giving freely of their time to help others. These were full-time, paid members of staff whose job it was to be able to communicate effectively.

It was simple really: I have rare skills that I was offering to use to help their girls. Surely, that's a positive thing - but not to them it wasn't! They prevaricated, they delayed, they behaved like total arseholes. Even when they understood perfectly well what I was saying, they pretended that they did not. They conveniently misinterpreted my e-mails to suggest that I was the one being awkward.

They kept mentioning their 'safeguarding policy' - as if they were trying to imply that I must be some sort of paedophile and hoping this would be enough to scare me off. (I don't know what concerns about paedophilia would have to do with girls over sixteen anyway!)

They tied themselves in knots trying to come up with excuses to turn down what must have been one of the most potentially valuable offers they'd ever encountered.

Eventually, they gave up trying to rationalise their objections and prejudices and simply resorted to a blatant lie: They tried to make out that they had no vacancies for volunteers - even though they'd already acknowledged that they had. It was sheer mindless nastiness like you wouldn't believe.

Arrogant, fucking cunts! They hated the idea of dealing with an intelligent person. They hated the idea of acknowledging my skills in any way, despite some of these skills having been clearly demonstrated in the course of our correspondence. Frankly, I think they'd have actually preferred to have a paedophile volunteering with them!

I made a complaint. It went up the chain of

command - and each person in the chain refused to acknowledge any mistakes whatsoever in the way my enquiries had been dealt with. As to my offer of help, they reinforced the message that my help was not wanted, but totally refused to explain this nonsensical position - how could they?

When cunts like these choose to remain stupid, that's one thing - I can laugh that off - but when they are so arrogant, so conceited and so obstructive that they abuse their position by denying opportunities for new generations to discover intelligence and freedom, that really does make me angry.

These cunts need to be cleaned from the streets. I want to kill them - and the damnable thing is that there doesn't seem to be a convincing, logical, rational reason why I shouldn't or why they don't deserve it!

I have two particular members of staff in mind. Either one will do to start with. I'll give it a while, then I'll turn up, catch one of them at an unsuspecting moment and knife her in the throat. What fun! I'm really looking forward to it. I was thinking of emigrating anyway.

I offered my help. I offered my time. I offered the skills I'd built up over decades of hard work. I offered kindness and I just got sneered at, viewed with suspicion and treated with contempt.

Oh, the sheer joy at seeing the look of utter surprise on their faces as they turn and see what's coming to them - surprise, even though they've been asking for it and asking for it with every sneering comment they've made! Fucking cunts!

# Illiteracy

A widespread lack of intelligence is hardly surprising given that most people can't even read or write any more. Our society is plagued by illiteracy. I'm not talking about the confusion about 'less' and 'fewer' or about misplaced apostrophes or people boldly splitting infinitives - I'm talking about a widespread basic inability to read and write.

OK, so most people can actually read...in a sense! They can read individual words. They may even have a good idea about some entire sentences - but most would struggle to properly digest the meaning in an article or even a paragraph that attempted to convey anything more than the simplest idea or concept.

People can sometimes judge the 'tone' or the 'gist' of something - although, very often, they get that wrong too - but as to precisely understanding what it actually says in black and white; fucking forget it!

People are crap at communicating! We have e-mailing, texting, twittering, web-chats and social networking - but the immediacy and proliferation of communication channels seems only to encourage people to be lazy cunts.

Even when people have something worth saying (a rarity these days!) and can be bothered to be reliable with their communications, they usually don't have the skills or the concentration to be precise in what they write or to take in the precise details of what they read. And I'm not just talking about Joe the train driver or Melissa on the checkout - I'm also referring to millions of people whose ability to efficiently perform their jobs fundamentally relies on their ability to understand and compose clear English.

Suppose you have an issue you wish to raise with your local council or with a department of central government. Imagine that you write a clear and precise letter or e-mail to the relevant member of staff. If your point is even slightly complex or involves any degree of subtlety, then the chances are high that the person you are writing to will fail to grasp the exact meaning of what you have written. This is despite the fact that they are supposed to be able to deal with such written communications as a major part of their everyday professional duties.

Very often, the member of staff, if they bother to write back to you at all, will ask for information which you have already provided or which clearly has nothing to do with the point you are trying to raise. Sometimes, they'll have managed to identify the general gist of what you have written, but will require a series of further correspondence before they can narrow down what exactly your point is - if, indeed, they ever manage to do so!

People are so used to face-to-face and phone conversations during which they can continually clarify what is being said, that they are unused to having to express themselves precisely in clear English the first time around.

And when someone else writes a clear and precise letter or e-mail to them, they're so fucking lazy and ignorant that they'll trot off some ill-considered response without having the manners or good sense to fucking-well properly read what was written to them in the first place. The very concept of being able to consistently and accurately express and understand precise points in clear written English is probably beyond them.

Our societies are mired in absurd bureaucracy and corporate inefficiency. Most of the bureaucratic activity we waste resources on is only required because of the widespread inability or refusal of people to learn to use English properly.

A large proportion of all meetings, presentations, video conferencing sessions, training sessions and business trips are only necessary because people are no longer able or prepared to communicate effectively through the simple written word - which, if used properly, would usually be the most efficient and effective form of communication. Imagine the joy at finding out that, "The training course is cancelled because we've simply cut through all that PowerPoint bullshit and summed up what you need to know on a single side of A4!"

Even leaving aside all the spam, most e-mails would be unnecessary if people had the skills to precisely express themselves and accurately understand each other in the first place.

We've spent thousands of years developing a fantastically wonderful system of communication. It's the English language - and written English in particular. One of the great things about the English language is that it provides a rich variety of interesting ways to describe the thieving bastards who claim wages from businesses, or even from public funds, despite being completely unable to perform, with any reasonable degree of effectiveness, the functions they're employed to perform. They can't perform these functions effectively because these cunts can't be fucking-well arsed to learn the language they are supposed to be using.

I'd like to waylay some of these cunts in a quiet

78

corner of an infrequently used alley and see if a large calibre gun to their heads will help them understand plain English! "You want to know what I want? Try actually reading the fucking letter I sent you months ago, you lazy, ignorant cunt! Ooops! Too late!"

# Bureaucrats

I'd love to go on a killing spree and take out some of the petty-minded bureaucrats who love being obstructive cunts, who love treating people like shit, but who think they can be immune to any backlash because they can hide behind their precious rules and regulations and the institution they work for.

These bureaucrats refuse to accept any responsibility for being arseholes, because the rules and regulations stipulate that they must behave like arseholes - and that's their defence. In actual fact, they often invent 'policies' specifically so that they can be arsy. When they refuse to be helpful or cooperative and you challenge them to justify their absurd position, they just send you one of those snotty little letters or e-mails saying, "It's not our policy to....." - as if that's the end of the matter. They refuse to give any rational or moral justification for this 'policy,' or any information about who is responsible for this 'policy' or where this 'policy' came from.

These petty bureaucrats - they're the ones I'd most like to drag screaming into the streets in order to execute the motherfucking cunts - preferably for as minor a crime as is reasonably excusable! I'd love to make these cunts suck on a shotgun before I blow their fucking brains out -

although I suspect you'd actually have to shoot them up the arse to achieve that!

Sure, I'd like to kill the big cheeses with overall responsibility for the rules and regulations, but, even more, I want to make the petty bureaucrats pay. The little cunts who think they can hide - so much more satisfying to kill them, because they love being awkward little cunts, but they think they can't be blamed for it. I want them most of all - and I want them to suffer, the fucking cunts!

Not so long ago, I killed a school secretary - a headteacher's secretary in fact. After I'd left teaching full-time and moved to a different part of the country, I wrote to the school where she worked to offer my expertise to their students. It was one of several schools I contacted, offering to help out on a voluntary basis. It seemed to me that my input would be of particular value to their brighter and more inquisitive students. What can I say? I like to help people!

This school did say on their website; "We're keen to foster close links with the community." What they actually mean, of course, is that they seek links that provide them with 'positive publicity.' As far as they are concerned, 'links with the community' refers to the occasional facile joint publicity venture with a well-known supermarket, bank or fast-food outlet. They want some pictures in the local paper and something each of the managers involved can use to further their greasy climb up the career ladder.

They want to look like they 'foster close links with the community' whilst all the time doing their damnedest to keep real members of the community at arm's length or even further. Partnerships with morally-repugnant corporations are fine, but if Mr. Bloggs down the road wants to offer his help and involvement, it is made abundantly clear to him that he is not wanted - Sod off! His kind offer of help is interpreted to be nothing but a front for paedophilia.

This particular secretary, like many of the others, ignored my initial e-mail and the first couple of reminders. She eventually responded, after a fashion, to one of my e-mails. Her response, however, contained no sort of apology for the delay caused by her previous failure to respond, or for the inconvenience of my having had to send her reminders.

Having finally acknowledged her own existence, she then made several thoroughly gutless and obstinate attempts to avoid answering my perfectly reasonable queries.

Exposing the appalling bigotry of these cunts is a simple matter. "Do you welcome volunteers from the local community offering their expertise to help your students?" I asked in my very first e-mail. What could she write in answer to such a simple and reasonable question?

She could hardly say no - that would totally contradict the stated policies of the school, the local authority and the government and could lead to disciplinary action - but she certainly didn't want to say yes, since that would sound like an invitation when what she really wanted to say was, "Fuck off!"

So, instead of answering my question, she responded with impertinent questions of her own, essentially asking why the hell I was bothering her when she had plenty of pointless paperwork she'd rather be getting on with. And she repeatedly mentioned their 'safeguarding policies' and 'vetting procedures' as if she was sure I had something to hide and that the very mention of security checks would see me running for the border! She treated me with increasing suspicion, not because there was any real reason to be suspicious, but simply because I had the impertinence to point out that she was totally failing to do her job properly and answer my perfectly reasonable questions.

Why was she treating me so badly, I asked, when all I had done was to contact the school out of the kindness of my heart, to offer my help and my specialist expertise? She liked being obstructive, but she didn't like me pointing out that she was being obstructive. So, having managed no more than intermittent, supercilious and thoroughly insincere semi-politeness at best, she decided to fall back on the strategy of simply ignoring my e-mails entirely.

She wasn't able to ignore me indefinitely, however. I left it a while before following her home one night. I put her under surveillance. I learnt her routes, her routines and her habits. I studied her personal relationships and engineered a convenient little dispute with her 'partner.' The source of their arguments and of her discontent became known to their friends and colleagues.

I killed her with a home-made captive bolt gun after a little more than an hour of joyous fun and games. Her body was never found - she remains just a missing person whose bank card has been used to withdraw occasional sums on the continent.

Fucking cunt - I thought I'd never have such fun again! I laughed so much it hurt. "Go on - say 'safeguarding policy' again you fucking bitch! SAY IT!" I made her say it over and over. She cried and sobbed it out again and again and I laughed heartily at her every time she did so. It was as she was saying it for the last time that I finally unleashed the bolt into her fucking brains!

That's what they do to you, these fucking people - they piss you off and push you and push you until they finally turn you into someone who enjoys this shit! They think they're immune, these petty bureaucrats, and they enjoy their feeling of immunity, the smug little cunts - but they're not immune; not from me!

## Stress

A common quote about the Vietnam War is that whilst fifty-five thousand US servicemen died in Vietnam, more then twice that number of veterans have since committed suicide. The same sort of thing happened with the Falklands War.

It is commonly assumed or asserted that these suicides were the result of the horrors of war and combat and the subsequent Post-Traumatic Stress Disorder that the veterans suffered from - but were they? Weren't many of them actually due to the shittiness of everyday civilian life?

In the armed forces, these veterans had real friends - people who took bullets for them. Back in civilian life, however, if they try to stand up for anything, they get treated like shit by people who will stab you in the back for the most ridiculously petty little thing.

They try to get a job and get treated abysmally by some anally-retentive interviewer who sneers at their lack of experience in the 'high-pressure' world of commerce.

They have to sign on at the job centre and are

made to sign a 'back-to-work contract,' and subject themselves to regular 'back-to-work interviews,' during which they have to repeatedly prove to some pointless state bureaucrat that they have the commitment to try to find a menial, underpaid job in some place where they will be treated like shit.

They have to demean themselves to prove to a pointless bureaucrat that *they* are not spongeing off the state. They have to go through pointless and degrading tick-box bureaucratic exercises to show their 'commitment' when they've been in the firing line, put their lives on the line and taken injuries. They must look at the shitty people they have to deal with and wonder why they bothered.

These veterans can no longer stand such sickening behaviour all around them - but can't give these shits the justice they deserve without going to prison (or to the chair) themselves. Isn't this often what really lies behind their post-traumatic stress?

# Distrust and Suspicion

A young girl walks into a playground, on her own, and starts playing on the equipment. Barely a minute later, when a mother and her children walk in, the little girl leaves the playground enclosure and just hangs around nearby. When the mother and her children leave the playground about fifteen minutes later, she immediately returns and starts playing on the slide and climbing frame again.

Did her parents tell her to behave this way, or is it, perhaps, that the general atmosphere of distrust and suspicion is so great that children don't have to be told - they just take it on board as normal? If the former is true, that's bad enough. If the latter is true, then our society is disintegrating - and may actually be in the final stages of collapse.

# Bomber Harris

Arthur 'Bomber' Harris was in charge of RAF Bomber Command for much of the Second World War. He was famous (or, as some would have it, infamous) for his 'They sowed the wind' speech.

Harris advocated and implemented an 'area bombing strategy' - put a little less hygienically; the carpet bombing of German cities. Perhaps most horrifically, 'thousand-bomber raids' were used to drop incendiary devices which, with favourable weather conditions, were able to create a firestorm - a fire that caused such an updraft and drew in so much oxygen that temperatures were high enough to melt people to the roads and pavements where they stood. People in bomb shelters suffocated because the air they were breathing had been depleted of all its oxygen. On some occasions, such as with the famous raid on Hamburg, tens of thousands died in a single night.

Today, it seems to be popular in certain quarters to deride Harris as some sort of war criminal, intent upon the mass murder of civilians - intent upon genocide. They like to make people believe that area bombing was both barbaric and entirely unnecessary.

"..And now they are going to reap the whirlwind!" was what Harris said as he sought to wipe German cities off the face of the Earth. Chilling words indeed, but I don't believe Bomber Harris was a nasty or callous man at all. In fact, I think he was a person who considered things very carefully. He simply considered that there was no point fighting a war half-heartedly and that to do so was supreme folly that would ultimately entail far worse consequences and far more deaths than would prosecuting the war efficiently and decisively in the first place.

It would be perfectly accurate to describe him as an extremely hard man - certainly not someone you would want to mess with - but it is totally unfair to deride him (as many people do) as some sort of callous maniac intent upon a murderous course with no point.

Harris was not, in any case, responsible for the decision to bomb Germany. Such decisions were made by politicians. The situation they faced was that, on the western front, we were not properly prepared for the Normandy landings until 1944 - and until D-Day arrived, there were only limited choices about how to attack Germany. We could hardly sit back and do nothing as millions were being killed repelling Hitler's barbaric campaigns of extermination on the Eastern Front and whilst millions more were worked to death in labour camps or being exterminated in the gas chambers.

We could and did engage in peripheral battles - such as in North Africa - but these engagements had limited effects in terms of degrading the Nazi war machine. It is all very well destroying tanks and other assets on the battlefield, but such strikes are of limited strategic value if the enemy can simply replace those assets. To substantially degrade the Germans' war-fighting capability and help the Soviets in their most desperate hour, we had to hit at Germany's production facilities - and that meant bombing.

Harris's job was not to decide whether or not to bomb Germany - that decision was made way above his head by Churchill and the war cabinet (although he is unlikely to have disagreed with it). He was simply told that he was to bomb Germany and his job was to make the bombing campaign as effective as possible.

If Harris could have chosen to bomb precision targets, doubtless he would have done so, but he did not have that choice. There was no laser-targeting or satellite guidance system! Bombs of the day were freefall munitions, aimed only by rough-guess-type aiming systems. Dropped from altitude and affected by the wind, they were capable only of being lobbed in the general direction of the enemy. Aiming at night was a science in its very early infancy. You could be more accurate by day, but then the losses you'd suffer from enemy fighters would be unsustainable - as the Germans had already discovered during the Battle of Britain.

The hard facts were that, early in the war, before Harris headed Bomber Command, ninety-seven percent of bombs missed their intended targets by five miles or more. The truth was that the RAF at the time simply did not have the capability to hit precision targets.

You could take the insincere get-out clause and say you were trying to bomb precision targets, whilst knowing all along that you simply didn't have the technology to actually hit precision targets. The bombs would still be killing people many miles away from the intended target - or they would fall relatively harmlessly into fields, perhaps killing a couple of cows. That might be fine in some people's eyes, except that tens of thousands of brave bomber crews would have died in a pointless endeavour that did nothing to shorten the war.

Someone who advocated or even insisted upon a precision-bombing policy might be retrospectively praised as a righteous man and moral campaigner

- but he would also have been an advocate of extreme folly. Saying the policy was precision bombing would have done nothing to change the reality. It would have been the coward's get-out clause!

Harris, however, did not falter in addressing his responsibilities or in facing up to the realities of war. He knew that the only targets he could effectively hit were the enemy's cities and large towns. Bombing might not break German morale (and it didn't), but industrial areas would be hit, housing would be destroyed and, just as importantly, munitions workers and others important to the German war effort, would be killed. There would be genuine and substantial disruption of production and some of the effort that would otherwise have been directed towards the Eastern Front would have to be redirected towards countering the bomber threat.

Yes, with bombing, innocent people would be killed, but without an effective bombing campaign that actually harmed Germany and disrupted production, the war would be prolonged, perhaps with millions of more deaths as a result. And for all Harris knew, a failure to hit the Germans where it hurt could even have changed the outcome of the war. Without the bombing campaign continually disrupting the German war effort, who knows what they might have achieved? After all, they got to within a few miles of Moscow.

Each time the Germans launched major offensives in the East, they suffered delays as they built up their forces and supplies. Campaigns planned for the spring or early summer were delayed until late summer or autumn. Before they knew it, they were fighting in the midst of a Russian winter and their cause was all but lost. Without the bombing campaigns disrupting production, the Nazis might have made it to Moscow or captured Stalingrad before the bad weather arrived.

We should also remember that Hitler had all sorts of hugely threatening advanced weapons programmes, including his own nuclear weapons programme. Perhaps, even undisturbed by bombing, he might not have got close to a nuclear weapon, but when you consider the V2 rocket technology they did develop that ultimately powered man to the moon, that was hardly a risk we could afford to take. We simply could not know for sure what sinister weapons he had in development and how close his weapons of mass destruction programmes were to fruition.

When decisions are made that result in unpleasant, undesirable or even deadly consequences, it is often easy to be glibly critical of those decisions without realistically considering what the options were. Very often, however, a bit of sober, intelligent analysis reveals that there were no nice, entirely desirable, pretty, rose-scented options available, as many people frequently seem to suppose there were. This is especially the case in war - yet many 'anti-war' campaigners conveniently seem to forget this simple fact. It's as if they think there was a nice, gentle way to deal with Hitler and his murderous hordes which, through some sort of carelessness, was mysteriously overlooked.

Britain in World War Two was fighting an all-out war. If any quarter were given to the Nazis, they would have used this breathing room to their advantage and to kill more people. At the very least, it would have meant an extended war; a delay in Germany's final defeat. This would have meant more deaths on the battlefields and more civilian deaths too, including in the gas chambers. The longer the war went on, the more people would be killed.

Harris simply sought to prosecute the war in the most effective way possible. He used his intelligence, he thought carefully about his strategy, but Bomber Harris did not have any nice options!

Several decades after the war, the much-loved Queen Mother unveiled a statue of Arthur Harris in London. She was horrified and had a look of utter bemusement and incredulity when she witnessed the ensuing protests against a man she certainly considered to be a war hero - a careful and considered man who sought to avoid unnecessary deaths and get the war won with as few casualties as possible. His only real crime was to have broken the modern laws of political-correctness fifty years before they were actually invented!

I'm with Bomber Harris. I'm not going to criticise him for picking unpleasant options. There simply were no nice or pleasant options available! The reality of life is that we often have to choose between alternative actions, all of which are undesirable to some extent. This doesn't mean we should be thoughtless or uncaring or aloof or indifferent to the consequences of our decisions or our actions. However, to refuse to make a choice and to do nothing simply because none of the alternatives are attractive, seems to me to be the most heinous crime of all.

"The Nazis entered this war under the rather childish delusion that they were going to bomb

everybody else, and nobody was going to bomb them. At Rotterdam, London, Warsaw, and half a hundred other places, they put that rather naive theory into operation. They sowed the wind, and now they are going to reap the whirlwind."
Arthur Harris

# Whirlwind

Hello. You don't know me, but I know you. You stupid fuck. You arrogant shit. You conceited piece of pus. You gutless, unprincipled lowlife. You conformist scum. You ungrateful cunt. You treat generosity with suspicion. You treat kindness with contempt. You want to know that people listen to you? Well, I listened to you. I listened to the sneering comments you made and I know exactly what sort of person you are. You want to know that someone is here for you? Well, I'm here for you. I'm here for you alright! Pain is here. Death is here. I'm here to rip you to pieces, you fucking cunt! I'm going to rip your whole fucking existence apart.

# Disgust

I view most other people as lower lifeforms. This is not out of prejudice or out of arrogance, but out of experience. Not for a minute does this mean that I assume the worst and treat people badly from the outset. In fact, I make a point of treating people with the utmost decency, but I am not naive and I refuse to be blind or indifferent to the uncomfortable reality that most people are not intelligent, alert, thinking human beings. The intelligent, decent person is the very rare exception in the cesspit of human existence.

## My Website:

To find out more about my work, including my other books, please visit **www.IMOS.org.uk**

Your comments on this book are welcome at: Rob@IMOS.org.uk

## Some of my other books:

Here is Wosdom
Seeking Wosdom
Pearls of Wosdom
Gifted
Whatever Happened to the Life of Leisure?
The Education of a Poker Player
Revelations: An Intelligent Analysis of Religious Beliefs

Printed in Great Britain
by Amazon